# Daddy
# Calls Me
# Man

A RICHARD JACKSON BOOK

# Daddy Calls Me Man

by ANGELA JOHNSON

*paintings by*
RHONDA MITCHELL

ORCHARD BOOKS

NEW YORK

Orchard Books, A Grolier Company, 95 Madison Avenue, New York, NY 10016

Manufactured in the United States of America
Printed and bound by Phoenix Color Corp.
Book design by Jennifer Browne

Hardcover 10 9 8 7 6 5 4 3 2
Paperback 10 9 8 7 6 5

The text of this book is set in 24 point Aldus.
The illustrations are oil paintings on canvas reproduced in full color.

Library of Congress Cataloging-in-Publication Data
Johnson, Angela.
Daddy calls me man / by Angela Johnson ; paintings by Rhonda Mitchell.
p.  cm.
"A Richard Jackson book"—Half t.p.
Summary: Inspired by his family experiences and his parents'
paintings, a young boy creates four poems.
ISBN 0-531-30042-0 (tr.)  ISBN 0-531-07175-8 (pbk.)
[1. Family life—Fiction. 2. Afro-Americans—Fiction. 3. Paintings—Fiction.]
I. Mitchell, Rhonda, ill. II. Title.
PZ7.J629Dah 1997  [E]—dc21  96-53865

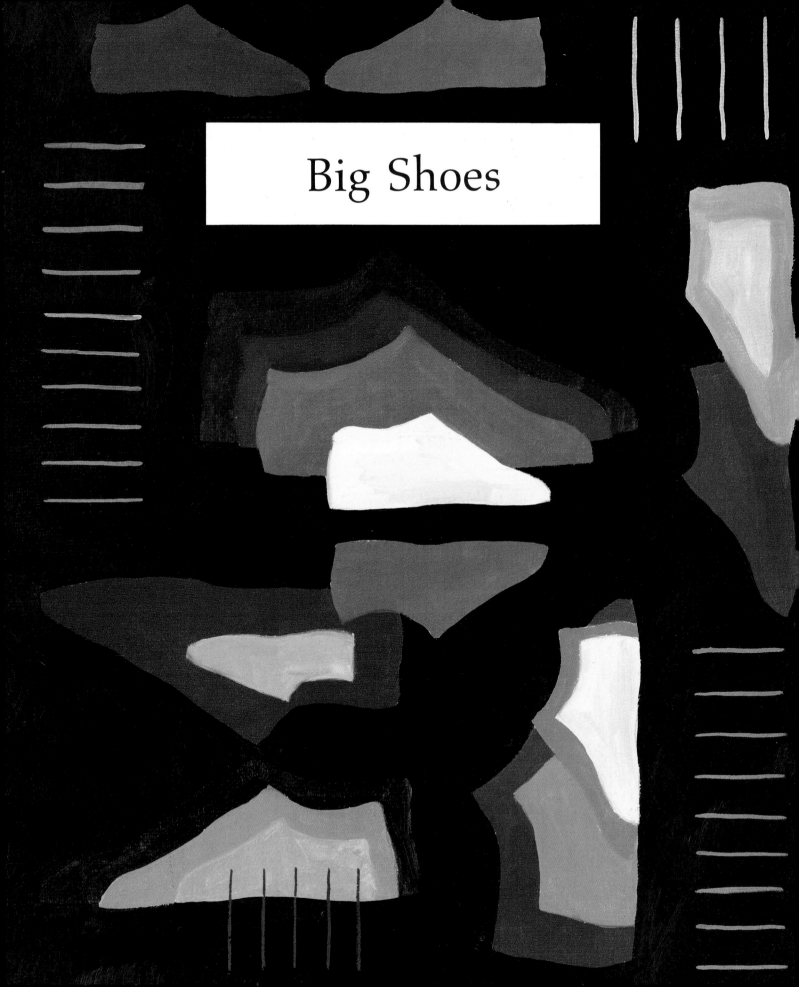

# Big Shoes

# All I want is big shoes

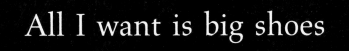

Red and black jump high shoes.

Line them up by Daddy's

and call them all our shoes.

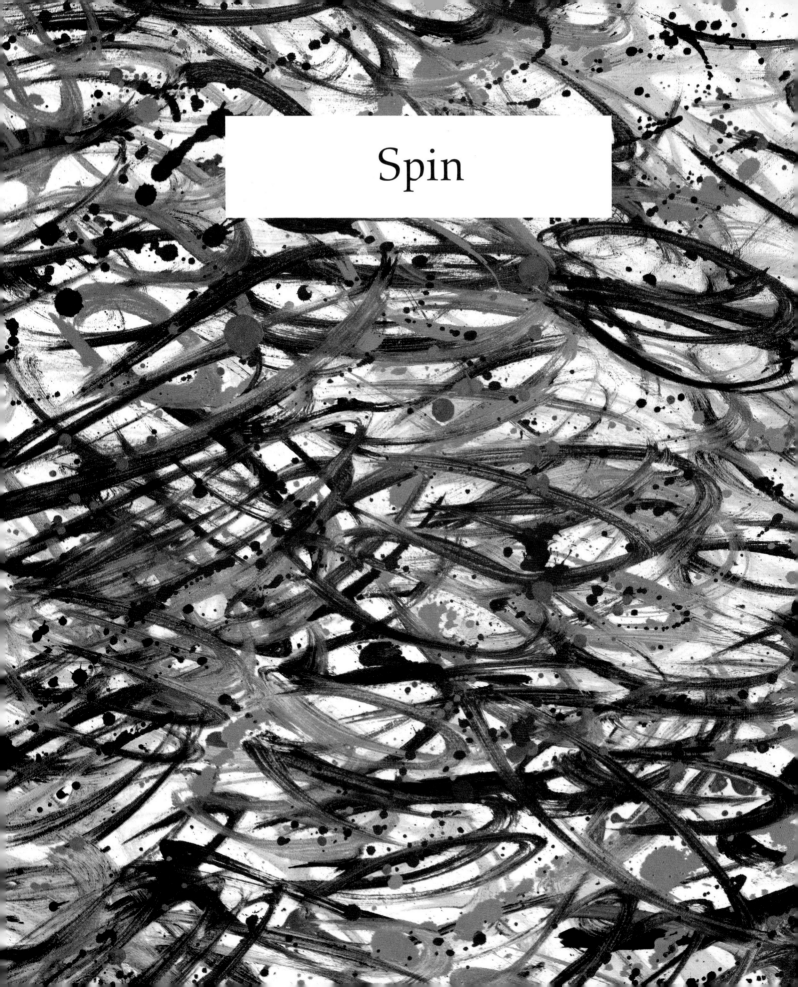

# Spin

Spin around the room.

Spin around the tree.

Swirl

Twirl

Spin and twist

Big sister and me.

# Noah's Moon

Mama calls it Noah's moon and says
it lives glowing in the sky.

Half a moon
Full moon

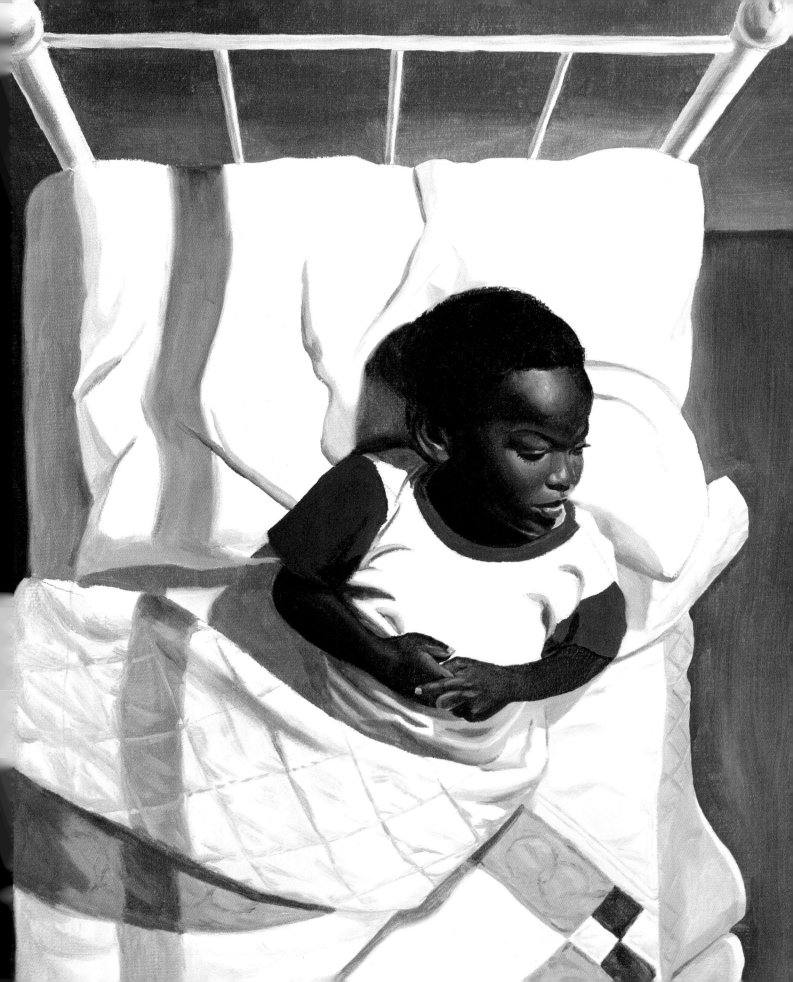

Me asking why.

Full moon, half moon
Glowing in the sky.

Baby Sister

Got a new baby sister
everybody comes to see.

Little bitty fingers
and smiles just for me.

I share toys
my room
and JoJo
anytime I can.

Then Mama calls me sweetheart

and Daddy calls me man.